LEAD THE WAY

By **Ace Landers**

Illustrated by **Garrett Taylor**

Inspired by the film

 PRESS

LOS ANGELES · NEW YORK

YOU always need SOMEBODY IMPORTANT in your life, SOMEBODY WHO . . .

To Dez, Wren, and Sterling. Pass it on.

Ace Landers

To my wife and best friend, Marybeth

Garrett Taylor

Editorial by **Eric Geron**
Design by **Winnie Ho**

Materials and characters from the movie *Cars 3*. Copyright © 2017 Disney Enterprises, Inc., and Pixar. All rights reserved.

Disney/Pixar elements © Disney/Pixar; rights in underlying vehicles are the property of the following third parties: Hudson, Hudson Hornet, Nash Ambassador, and Plymouth Superbird are trademarks of FCA US LLC; Dodge®, Jeep® and the Jeep® grille design are registered trademarks of FCA US LLC; FIAT is a trademark of FCA Group Marketing S.p.A.; Mercury is a trademark of Ford Motor Company; Chevrolet and Chevrolet Impala are trademarks of General Motors; Mack is a trademark of Mack Trucks, Inc.; PETERBILT and PACCAR trademarks licensed by PACCAR Inc., Bellevue, Washington, U.S.A.; Petty marks used by permission of Petty Marketing LLC; Carrera and Porsche are trademarks of Porsche; Sarge's rank insignia design used with the approval of the U.S. Army; Volkswagen trademarks, design patents and copyrights are used with the approval of the owner, Volkswagen AG; Background inspired by the Cadillac Ranch by Ant Farm (Lord, Michels and Marquez) © 1974.

Printed in the United States of America
First Hardcover Edition, April 2017
10 9 8 7 6 5 4 3 2 1
FAC-034274-17048
ISBN 978-1-4847-8127-2 (Trade edition)
ISBN 978-1-368-00908-9 (Barnes and Noble edition)
Library of Congress Control Number: 2016958413
Visit www.disneybooks.com

to show up and
WORK HARD.

Somebody who reminds you that when you can't do something right the **FIRST** time . . .

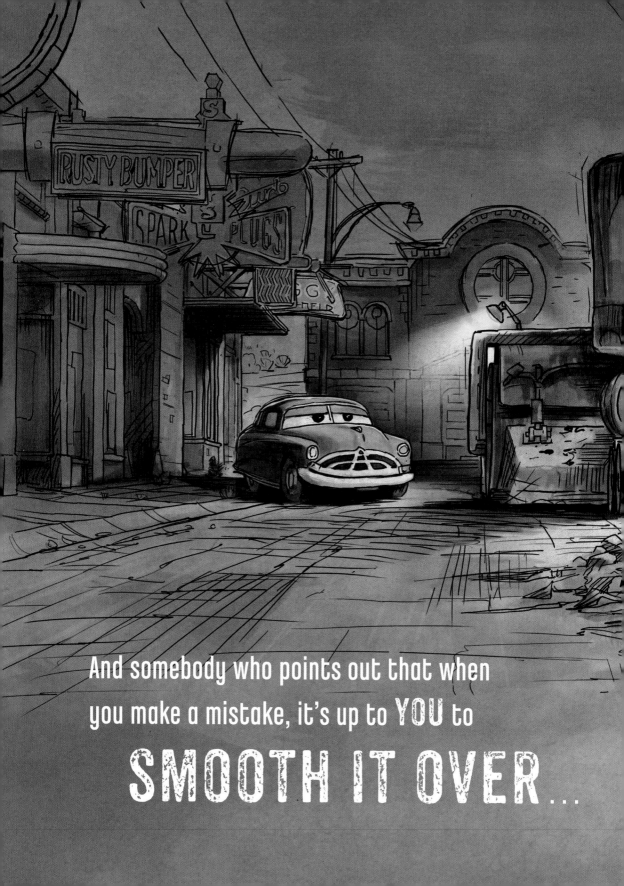

And somebody who points out that when
you make a mistake, it's up to YOU to
SMOOTH IT OVER...

even when there's a long road ahead.

You need that important somebody to show you that even when **YOU THINK YOU KNOW IT ALL,**

there's always **SOMETHING**
MORE TO LEARN.

SOMEBODY who teaches you . . .

that being **A TRUE**

CHAMPION

doesn't always mean winning . . .

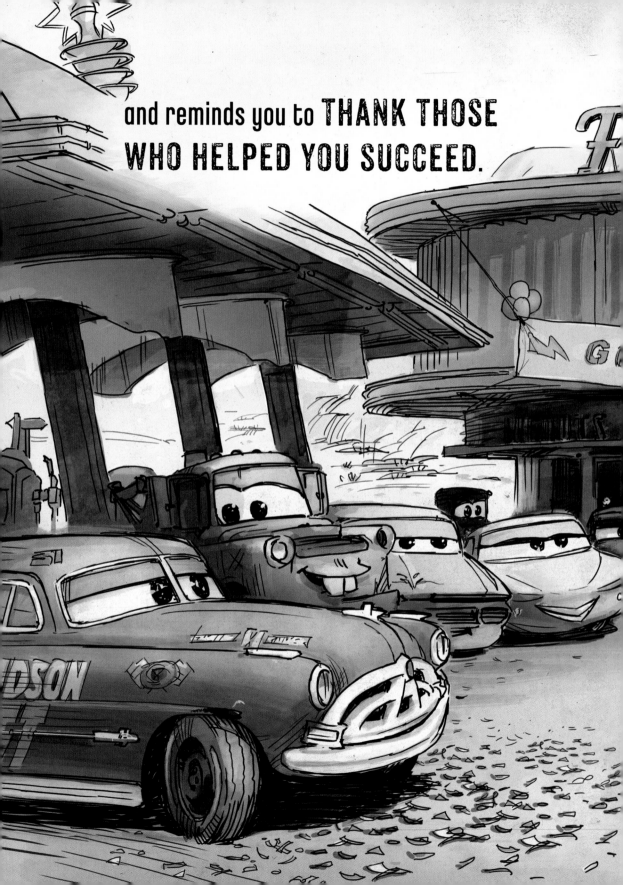

and reminds you to **THANK THOSE WHO HELPED YOU SUCCEED.**

You need that **DRIVING FORCE** of a **SOMEBODY** to demonstrate that when you're **UP AGAINST A WALL**, there's always **A CREATIVE WAY** to turn things around.

That's what an **IMPORTANT SOMEBODY**...

shows you on and off the track.

WHO KNOWS?

Maybe one day down the road you will find **SOMEONE** looking to **YOU** for guidance . . .

and you will have **SO MUCH TO SHARE.**

and BELIEVE
IN THE IMPOSSIBLE.

You will inspire that SOMEONE . . .

to **GIVE BACK** to others . . .

and you will show that someone how to

SHIFT GEARS

and have fun!

You will be there to
CROSS THE **FINISH** LINE
WITH THAT SOMEONE . . .

and prove that the trophy **ISN'T** the only reward. . . .

The **TRUE REWARDS** are the **FRIENDS** and **MEMORIES** you make along the way.